Hello, Family Members,

Learning to read is one of the most important accomplishments of early childhood. **Hello Reader!** books are designed to help children become skilled readers who like to read. Beginning readers learn to read by remembering frequently used words like "the," "is," and "and"; by using phonics skills to decode new words, and by interpreting picture and text clues. These books provide both the stories children enjoy and the structure they need to read fluently and independently. Here are suggestions for helping your child *before*, *during*, and *after* reading:

Before

- Look at the cover and pictures and have your child predict what the story is about.
- Read the story to your child.
- Encourage your child to chime in with familiar words and phrases.
- Echo read with your child by reading a line first and having your child read it after you do.

During

- Have your child think about a word he or she does not recognize right away. Provide hints such as "Let's see if we know the sounds" and "Have we read other words like this one?"
- Encourage your child to use phonics skills to sound out new words.
- Provide the word for your child when more assistance is needed so that he or she does not struggle and the experience of reading with you is a positive one.
- Encourage your child to have fun by reading with a lot of expression . . . like an actor!

After

- Have your child keep lists of interesting and favorite words.
- Encourage your child to read the books over and over again. Have him or her read to brothers, sisters, grandparents, and even teddy bears. Repeated readings develop confidence in young readers.
- Talk about the stories. Ask and answer questions. Share ideas about the funniest and most interesting characters and events in the stories.

I do hope that you and your child enjoy this book.

— Francie Alexander
  Reading Specialist,
  Scholastic's Learning Ventures

To Jordan
— Love, Mommy

For Edie Weinberg
— B.L.

**Go to www.scholastic.com for Web site information
on Scholastic authors and illustrators.**

Text copyright © 1999 by Grace Maccarone.
Illustrations copyright © 1999 by Betsy Lewin.
All rights reserved. Published by Scholastic Inc.
SCHOLASTIC, HELLO READER, CARTWHEEL BOOKS
and associated logos are trademarks and/or registered
trademarks of Scholastic Inc.

Library of Congress Cataloging-in-Publication Data

Maccarone, Grace.
 The class trip / by Grace Maccarone; illustrated by Betsy Lewin.
    p.   cm. — (First grade friends) (Hello reader! Level 1)
 "Cartwheel Books."
 Summary: When his class goes to the zoo, Sam fails to keep up with the rest of the group and gets lost.
 ISBN 0-439-06755-3
 [1. Zoos — Fiction.   2. Zoo animals — Fiction.   3. School field trips — Fiction.   4. Lost children — Fiction.   5. Stories in rhyme.]
 I. Lewin, Betsy, ill.   II. Title.   III. Series.   IV. Series: Maccarone, Grace. First grade friends.
 PZ8.3.M127Cj   1999   99-10687
 [E]—dc21   CIP
                                                            AC

12 11 10 9   0/0 01 02

Printed in the U.S.A.   24
First Scholastic printing, November 1999

The Class Trip

by Grace Maccarone
Illustrated by Betsy Lewin

Hello Reader! — Level 1

Cartwheel
·B·O·O·K·S·®

SCHOLASTIC INC.
New York Toronto London Auckland Sydney
Mexico City New Delhi Hong Kong

The teacher says,
"It's time to go."
So she puts on her hat
with the polka-dot bow.

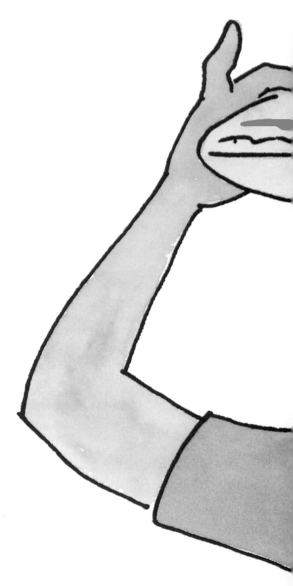

Then Sam, Jan, Pam,
Max, Kim, and Dan

get on the bus
as fast as they can.

They sit in seats
two by two.
They talk. They sing.

They're at the zoo.

Sam sees the chimps.
They fight. They play.

Sam's friends move on.
Sam wants to stay.

The teacher says,
"Sam, don't be slow.
Keep up with the group.
It's time to go."

Monkeys chatter.
They swing. They climb.

Sam is having
a wonderful time.

The teacher says,
"Sam, don't be slow.
Keep up with the group.
It's time to go."

Elephants walk.

Lions run.

Polar bears
enjoy the sun.
Sam is having
so much fun.

The teacher says,
"Sam, don't be slow.
Keep up with the group.
It's time to go."

Fish swim.

Frogs leap.

Flowers float.

Turtles sleep.

Sam looks up
and has a scare.
Sam is alone.
His group is not there!

Which way did they go?
Sam does not know.
He looks up high.
He looks down low.
Sam tries to stand
on tippy-toe.

And that's when he sees
the polka-dot bow.
Sam runs to his teacher.

Now he will know
to stay with his group
and go, go, go, GO!